by Lea Taddonio   illustrated by Mina Price

Head over Heels

First Kiss

Spellbound

An Imprint of Magic Wagon
abdopublishing.com

To PB &J, my favorite combo —LT

For Corinne & Tori —MP

abdopublishing.com

Published by Magic Wagon, a division of ABDO, PO Box 398166,
Minneapolis, Minnesota 55439. Copyright © 2017 by Abdo
Consulting Group, Inc. International copyrights reserved in all
countries. No part of this book may be reproduced in any form
without written permission from the publisher. Spellbound™ is a
trademark and logo of Magic Wagon.

Printed in the United States of America, North Mankato, Minnesota.
102016
012017

Written by Lea Taddonio
Illustrated by Mina Price
Edited by Heidi M.D. Elston
Art Directed by Candice Keimig
Series lettering and graphics from iStockphoto

Publisher's Cataloging-in-Publication Data

Names: Taddonio, Lea, author. | Price, Mina, illustrator.
Title: First kiss / by Lea Taddonio ; illustrated by Mina Price.
Description: Minneapolis, MN : Magic Wagon, 2017. | Series: Head over heels ; Book 4
Summary: Lola Jones is head over heels for her new boyfriend, C J Kline. But she's
   keeping a secret from him. She's never kissed anyone.
Identifiers: LCCN 2016947648 | ISBN 9781624021954 (lib. bdg.) | ISBN 9781624022555
   (ebook) | ISBN 9781624022852 (Read-to-me ebook)
Subjects: LCSH: High school students--Juvenile fiction. | Best friends--Juvenile fiction. |
   Interpersonal relationships--Juvenile fiction. | Human behavior--Juvenile fiction.
Classification: DDC [Fic]--dc23
LC record available at http://lccn.loc.gov/2016947648

Table
of
Contents

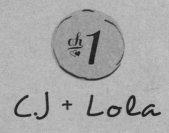

C.J + Lola

After my **DRUM LINE** rehearsal ends, I sit in the gym **bleachers** and wait for C.J to finish **BASKETBALL** practice. I draw **hearts** on my MATH homework to pass the time.

"What does that say?"

My **BEST FRIEND** Kizzie sneaks up behind me and reads what I wrote in the corner. "C.J plus Lola equals **FOREVER**?"

"**STOP** spying!" I hunch over the paper and **COVER** the words with my hand.

"Hey, girl. Don't get all *shy*." Kizzie sits and puts her arm *around* my shoulder. "I'm **happy** for you. **EVERYONE** agrees you two make a great *couple.*"

C.J sinks a three-pointer
and **waves** up at me.
His *smile* is so **cute**.

"I like him **A LOT**." I can't stop my *smile*. "He's a great guy."

Kizzie winks. "And I bet he's a great *kisser* too. Come on, give me the DETAILS."

My smile FADES.
Kizzie GASPS. "You
have **kissed** him, *right?*"

"Please be quiet." I tug down my knit cap and hope no one hears her. Does she have to have such a **BIG MOUTH**?

"Oh my gosh." She POKES my arm. "You **HAVEN'T**, have *you*?"

"No." I duck and **HUG** my chest. My **MOUTH** gets dry. "I've never **kissed** a boy."

There. I said it out loud. My deepest, *darkest* secret.

Never Been Kissed

C.J walks me **HOME** after his practice. The sky is **DARK** and *GLOOMY*.

"You're quiet tonight." He glances at my face and **frowns**. "What's *wrong*?"

"Guess I've got **A LOT** on my mind." Can he tell by **looking** at me that I've never been *kissed*? "Hold up." C.J **STOPS** and *takes* my hand. "You can be STRAIGHT with me."

But how can I admit that I don't have **ANY** idea how to **kiss**? What if he **laughs** at me? I feel so **STUPID**!

"Don't *worry*." I pull away. "It's no **BIG** deal." I start walking fast. My **CHEEKS** are **HOT**. I don't even know where I'm going. I just need to *MOVE*.

"Lola!" he calls. "*Wait.*"

I turn left into the **CITY** park. There are lots of **TREES**. I wish I could **CLIMB** the tallest one and *hide*.

C.J catches up. "You **NEED** to tell me what's going on."

I take a deep breath. "*Promise* not to **laugh**?" He **HUGS** me. "I'd *never* do that."

"Okay." I SQUEEZE my eyes shut. Here goes nothing. "I've never **kissed** anyone."

It's Our Kiss

C.J doesn't say a word. His **WHOLE** body is still. Thunder **rumbles** over our heads.

"I'm **sorry**," I whisper. "I don't know how to **kiss**."

"Don't do that, Lola." He puts a hand **under** my chin and *tilts* my head back. "Never apologize for who *you* are."

"Have you **kissed** lots of girls?" I bite the inside of my **CHEEK**. He's the school basketball star. He's probably **kissed** twenty girls.

27

"You are all that matters. When I **look** at you, it's like there's never been *anyone* else." C.J tucks a piece of my hair **BEHIND** my ear. "It's like there's never going to be *anyone* else. Not **EVER** again."

It starts RAINING. He shrugs
out of his VARSITY jacket and
holds it **over** our heads to
keep us dry. The world is gone.
It's only *him* and **me** in
this dark space.

"You've never even tried to **kiss** me." I feel **DUMB** saying this, but it's **TRUE**. "Not one time."

"You're right." He nods. "I *wanted* to take things **slow**."

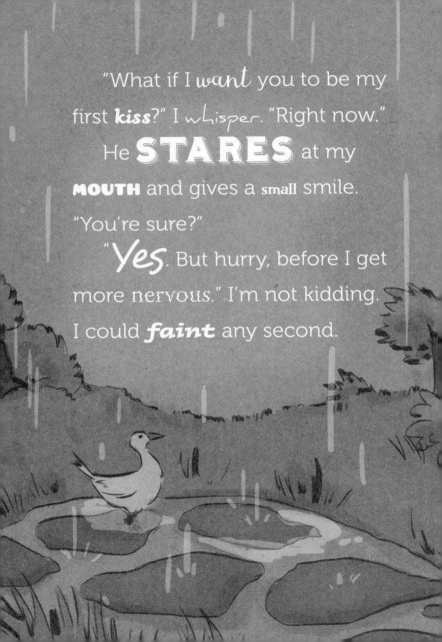

"What if I *want* you to be my first **kiss**?" I *whisper*. "Right now."

He **STARES** at my **MOUTH** and gives a small smile.

"You're sure?"

"**Yes**. But hurry, before I get more nervous." I'm not kidding. I could *faint* any second.

"Don't be," he says.

"What if it's the

WORST *kiss* ever?"

I ask.

"No way." His *smile*

gets **BIGGER**. "It

will be the ***BEST*** kiss.

Because it's **OUR** kiss."

Own Your Heart

"Ready?" C.J **CLOSES** his eyes. I do the same. "**Yes**. I'm ready." My hands **shake** as he bends down. Then it happens. His lips **brush** mine, **SOFT** and **gentle**. He tastes like **mint** gum.

Then he starts to pull away. But it's over too **FAST**! I **grab** his shoulders and tug him back. Rain FALLS around us, but I don't feel **COLD** or wet. I'm **warm** all over.

"**Wow**," he says when we stop. "That was like mågic."

"Was it okay?" I **touch** the side of his *face*.

His answer is another **kiss**. A *longer* one. My **heart** is louder than the **thunder**. He presses his forehead AGAINST mine. "I didn't know **kissing** could be like this."

I hold him TIGHT. He drops his jacket on the WET sidewalk and swings me off my feet. We are getting WET, but we don't care. We don't notice anything but each other.

"*Lola*," he says my name
like it's the **BEST** word ever.
"When I look at you, I feel like I
am looking at my FUTURE.
That's **crazy**, right?"

"I have the same sort of **crazy** *feeling*," I say.

He **SCOOPS** up his VARSITY jacket and puts it **over** my shoulders. "I don't want you to catch a **COLD**."

I rise on my toes and **PRESS** my *lips* to his again. I could get used to **kissing**. "You might own the basketball court," I whisper, "but I want to own your **heart**."